Meli's Journal

The Flight of Assilem

by

Melissa Anne Poteat

Walk upright and harm none.

George W Stevenson

Preface

Traveling to many different lands, Melinda took time to jot down different things that she saw at different occasions that she would get to experience. She felt that this would be a good way of documenting what she saw. She never intended anyone of reading her journals, but it was just something that she enjoyed doing after her adventures.

Assilem was Meli's land of air. Flight was always an enjoyment to her, not so much for Beast. His awkward puppy stage he was in made flying even more difficult for him. Many things were explored in this airy land; fowl, elements, and even some unusual creatures she had met in other lands.

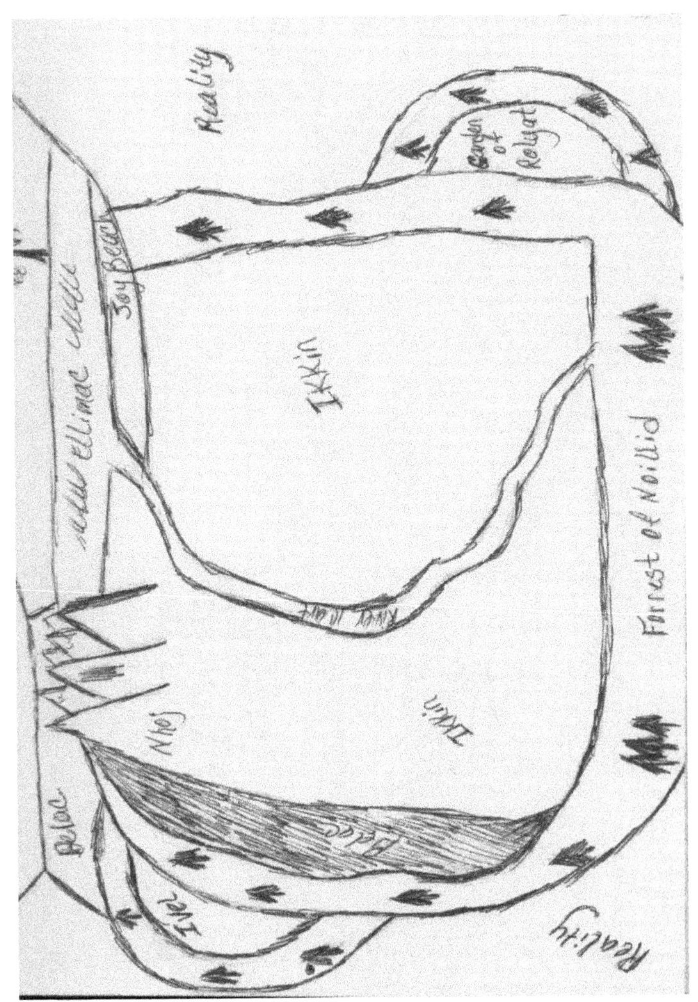
Reality
Garden of Rolyat
Joy Beach
Ellimac
Ikkin
Forrest of Noillid
Nhoj
Ikkin
Beloc
Beloc
Ivel
Reality

January

Assilem is a land like air. Well, that's because it's in the air. Above the high peaks of Nhoj lays the calm and peaceful land of clouds.

When Beast and I first arrived in this light as air place, I thought of how…nice; peaceful but boring. Ikkin is my land of happy thoughts and rejuvenation, but did I have two lands like that?

No!

Walking through the clouds, and kicking them just for fun as we walked, the tranquility was disrupted when something went buzzing past my head. It was a flying leafer. Before too long

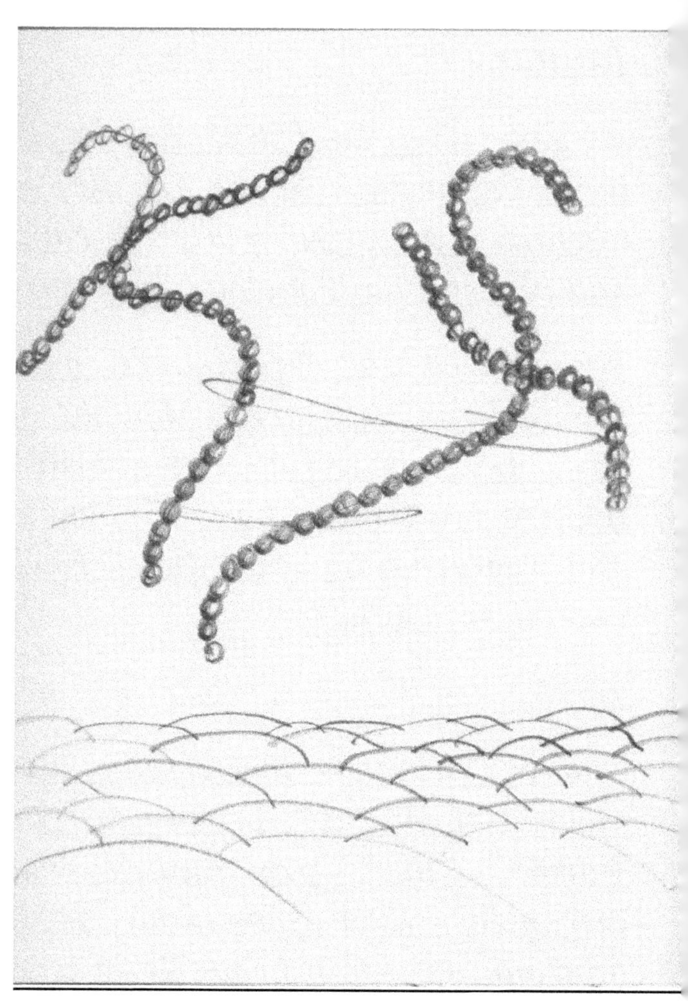

There were several fluttering around spreading their blue glitter dust.

I sat down on the pillowy substance. Beast sat next to me without making a sound. He just had this curious look on his face like he does in reality when his brain is distributing information.

The leafers were busy little guys. I was not sure exactly what they were up to but we just sat and watched with expectation. And we were not let down.

Just as the clouds move and make different shapes in the sky, the leafers glitter was doing the same thing. I then realized they were entertaining us with their shapes, creatures, moons, stars and birds.

Back in reality, I looked up towards the heavens to view the clouds. Thinking of the images the flying leafers had given us; I could not help but wonder if there was any significance to them. Were they trying to tell us something?

February

When you think of clouds, you normally think of snow clouds, thunder storm clouds, and rain clouds. Assilem's clouds were a grouping of sturdy fluff.

The first day we went to Assilem the clouds were white, today they were pink. It made me think of balls of cotton candy. As tempting as it was, I did not lick them to see if they tasted like the sugary air. I had hoped Beast would not slobber on them just in case; I would hate to think that we were responsible for melting an entire land. It did not happen so when we left the land it was still in tact.

The leafers were not there to greet us today. I figured they must have had something to do. However, we

did walk up on a great wall of clouds. Beast and I walked all around trying to find a door or some way of getting through. I finally told Beast we could probably just walk through them. Beast stepped back as if he was too chicken to go first so I pressed my hands against one portion of the wall. My hands went straight through it.

I told Beast it was ok. He still seemed to be timid about going through it so I just stepped right on through.

So I found out that this was not the brightest thing I had ever done when I found myself dangling over the Mountains of Nhoj. There I was hanging on to a cloud with one *hand screaming for Beast to get me. Well I should hand known he wasn't going to come through the wall with me screaming since he was hesitant about the whole thing anyways; he didn't.*

He did however grab the end of the rope that I called for and helped pull me back through the wall. This showed me two things. One, if Beast is hesitant about something pay attention to him, and two, don't go through walls without looking first.

March

Today was crazy when we arrived in Assilem today. The wind was blowing pretty hard. I think Beast was wishing he had stayed home and napped. The clouds were black which made me wonder just what was happening. Of course I automatically thought there must be a demon nearby. It was strange though. The leafers were flying about like they were not worried, but the blackness in the sky did have me worried.

Suddenly the clouds shook as a rumbling sound rolled across the area. Beast hunkered down onto the clouds. I sat down beside of him. I *had learned my lesson to watch his reactions. The*

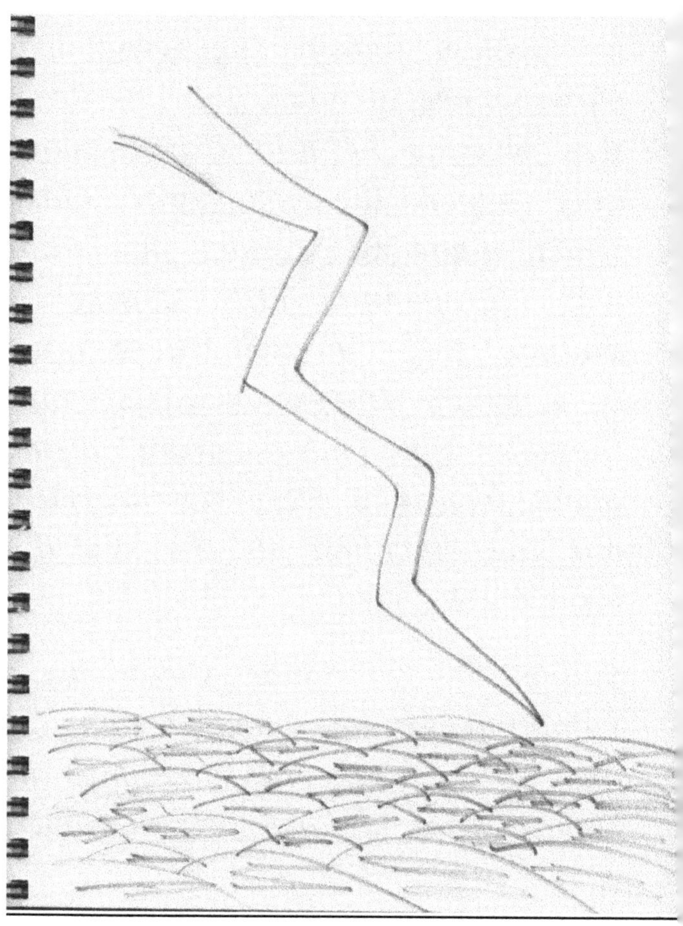

leafers came to where we were. One even landed on Beast's nose as if he was trying to comfort him. One landed on my shoulder and whispered in my ear to watch; so I did.

It was amazing what happened next. It was a light show like I had never seen before. Now I know in reality lightening is a dangerous thing and I would never think of being outside during a thunder storm, but the leafers seemed at ease with the flying electricity so I figured all was good; and it was.

One strike after another flew above the cloud floor, through the cloud floor, and around the cloud floor.

Then the most amazing thing happened. The leafers all flew at once into the air. A streak of lightening flew and the leafers flew into it. At first I was freaking out. I jumped up with panic in my heart. I had no idea what to do or why they would even to such a thing. As I watched with tears in my eyes, I realized that the leafers were playing in the lightening. With every strike it was like they received more energy and pep.

Just a quickly as the storm had come, it left. The leafers flew back down to where Beast and I were. They flew in a circle in front of us. There were so many of them we couldn't really see what they were *doing. Finally they disburse and flew off in different directions.*

One leafer stayed behind. He flew up to me and sustained in mid-air. He had a little brown suede leather pouch in his mouth. I held my hand out for him to place the pouch in it. I told him thank you and he flew away.

I opened the pouch to find that it was filled with the blue glittery powder. I thought of how honored I felt that they would give me such a gift.

April

The land of Assilem was loud today. Beast decided not to come and I think he may have made the right decision.

The noise was from the thousands of birds that were there. It was like I had stepped into an Alfred Hitchcock movie. The birds were not aggressive or anything; just flying around and sitting all around the clouds.

There were big birds, small birds, multi-colored birds, black birds, and loud birds. It was a bit insane.

One bird flew towards me and landed on my shoulder. I said hello; as if it was going to answer me back. Well, it did. She was a small blue bird with sparkling blue eyes.

She told me her name was Deb. She was headed to Joy Beach. I asked her if all the birds were headed to the beach and she said that they all had different places to be. Assilem was a type of pit stop for them. I asked her what they did during this pit stop. She said they would all just chat with each other and talk about where they had come from and their plans of where they were headed. She said that she was headed to Joy Beach to spend a couple days there and then she was headed to The Garden of Rolyat. She told me that the grapes were ripe and she always likes to nest down there during the picking season.

I told her I had been in Assilem a few times and I had never seen any birds until today. She said that

there were only certain days Assilem opened up for them. She had heard that because of all the squawking and chattering the land could only handle them every now and then. I told her I did not mean to be rude, but I could understand why. She said that the leafers always opened the land up to them whenever they were not going to be there.

Back in my reality I saw a group of birds in the woods behind the house. I wondered if they had stopped at Assilem, or if they had an Assilem to stop at.

May

Today Beast and I arrived in Assilem early. The cloud ground was a mix of orange and red. This was unusual but beautiful. I noticed that there was a brightness that seemed to be shinning through the fluffed pillows we were walking on. I ran to the great wall of clouds and stuck my head through to see what was going on. I thought there may be trouble in Nhoj or one of the other lands. I did not see anything unusual so I ran to another part of the wall.

This time when I stuck my head through, I was greeted with the biggest, brightest, and hottest ball ever.

Yes, we had arrived at sunset.

I quickly pulled my head back and ran back to where Beast was standing waiting patiently. I ran past him and told him he might want to back up a bit.

The cloud ground shook as the sun made its way through the clouds. It was amazing, but at the same time a bit scary.

It was not long before it had past through and the land was back to normal.

June

Today in Assilem Beast and I were greeted with a very unusual sight. I had never really thought of this land having a moon, but when you think about it, all lands have a moon.

Assilem's moon was spectacular. It was one moon made up of three quarter moons. When we view our one moon made up of one moon in reality, the shadows allow us to view the moon in quarters and halves. In this land there were no shadows. The moon was actually cut out this was as if it had been cut out with a cookie cutter.

The low hanging piece of artwork intertwined in and out of itself. It was like watching a mechanical

piece in motion. It was pretty spectacular. Even Beast got a kick out of watching it.

July

Nights in Assilem are so relaxing. I had propped my head up on Beasts back as he laid curled up behind me. Lying on the clouds is like nothing I had ever experienced.

We were so relaxed I heard Beast snoring at one point so I reached around and petted his head and told him that he was missing the view. He looked up towards the multitude of stars and then laid his head back down on the cloud pillow he had gathered up with his paws.

That was fine; I enjoyed the twinkling lights that were right over our heads.

Looking up, I noticed that the stars were not like our stars in reality. It was like they were alive looking back at me. Then I saw that they were not only looking at me, they were whispering to each other. I could not help but think, are they relaxing watching me and Beast watching them?

My curiosity got the best of me. I had to see if my suspicion were true. I stood up and reached as high as I could to see if I could touch one of them. Not being able to, I jumped up. Not realizing the clouds being so fluffy made them a bit springy, I jumped higher than I had expected.

With my yelp, Beast jumped up from where he was laying to see what was going on. Just as he did, I came plummeting down on his head. A little confused, he thought I was playing with him, so he pounced on me before I could get up. I pushed him off of me and just as I stood up, here he came at me again. I told him "ok buddy, you asked for it".

Using the springy clouds, I leaped over him and quickly turned around. He had been sleeping so he did not realize why I could do this.

After a bit of wrestling around with him and leaping over him, we tuckered ourselves out and took a small nap.

I never did find out what the stars were whispering about. I suppose that will be another adventure.

August

In life a little rain must fall, or in the case of Assilem, rise. That was what Beast and I found today.

The clouds were sloppy wet; they squished underneath my boots. I could tell Beast was not too happy about getting his feet wet. They were not wet from rain falling down on them and it was a little strange because droplet of water seemed to be rising from the wet cloud underneath our feet.

Curious to see what was going on, I went to the great wall to look out over the other lands. They looked fine. No rain in any of them. I finally thought that since the moisture was coming from under us

I would pull back some of the clouds we were standing on.

I carefully stuck my hands in the wet mushy fluff. The wetness made it difficult because of their weight. When I finally got through, water droplets by the hundreds flew up into my face. They got Beast too because he had his big nose in the way.

The flying leafers came and started flutter around. It then dawned on me what was going on. The clouds were drawing water as they prepared for a storm. The leafers were all gathering for their lightening dance.

September

Today in Assilem Beast and I were walking around exploring different areas of the clouded land when we heard a crow caw. I knew this was not a bird day because there were none here so we hurried to the great wall, where the sound was coming from. Just as we reached it, this huge crow came flying through it, knocking me backwards. I sure am glad that the clouds are soft because that surely would have left a bruise.

When I got to my feet and regained my composure, Beast was barking at the huge black bird. He gets aggressive when it comes to protecting me. He's a good friend.

I noticed that the black bird was not alone. He actually had a rider. I

called for my sword just in case there was trouble.

I lowered my dagger when I saw that it was just Noillid. It is pretty cool that he is able to cross from land to land, but I do wish he would warn me when he is entering the land I am in.

He said he was flying around and heard me and Beast so he thought he would stop by and say hello; so he said hello and hopped back on the crow and flew away.

He is a strange little guy, but I guess if I was from the land of beauty and was cursed because of being too curious I too would be strange. It is nice to know that he does check in on me. Just like in reality, friends *are hard to come by and even though Noillid is a grumpy little man, I consider him to be my friend. If truth be known, I think he feels the same.*

October

I was really glad to be back in Assilem today. I had been thinking about being in a land of the air. Everything here either flies, floats, or hovers. I had wondered if Beast and I could, so today was the day we were going to try it.

It took a little convincing when it came to Beast letting loose of the ground, but after letting him know that I would try it first.

I took a deep breath and jumped into the air and came back down just as quick. I decided to take a run and go so I took off running as fast as I could and...jumped...and fell into the clouds. Then I heard a small voice say "you have to concentrate".

I looked around not seeing anything that had said that. I asked Beast if he had learned to talk; he barked.

After trying a couple more time and having the same results, the voice said once again, “you have to concentrate”.

I asked who was saying that when one of the fluffy clouds giggled underneath my feet, causing my foot to vibrate. I asked the clouds why they had not spoken to me before and in unison a thousand small voices said, “We're concentrating”.

Well of course they were.

I took a deep breath and closed my eyes to concentrate on flying and making my body light as a feather.

In just a moment or two I felt my body lift slowly into the air. I opened one eye to peek out to see if I was truly floating; I was. Beast barked and I told him he needed to concentrate.

The feeling to being so light was like no other. The clouds whispered, "That's it". I opened my other eye and started guiding my body with my mind in which direction I wanted to go. It was incredible. I am so jealous of the birds now.

I think Beast is jealous of me because he never would concentrate.

November

Beast and I entered Assilem a bit late today thanks to Beast chasing what he obviously thought was a cat in our reality. I know dogs do this, but when I have to give him a bath because the cat turned out to be a skunk; really. Needless to say I was a bit aggravated with him.

The sight in the airy land today was worth the wait though. Just as the sun rises, it also settles and we were just in time to witness this.

It was half way past when we entered. We stayed back a ways so that we would not be blinded by its brightness but as soon as it had lowered itself under the clouds, we ran to the great wall and peeked out over the lands.

The sun slowly moved downward towards Ellimac, where it settled into its watery bed. It was a pretty awesome sight.

After the crazy day I had with Beast and his adventure, it was nice to end the day with such a comforting sight. I guess that is like life, sometimes you really don't have to look that hard to find comfort. It could come from a sunset, a rainy day, or even a cup of coffee sitting on the front porch. I think I understand why my grandmother loved doing that now.

I sat down beside of Beast and told him not to worry about the skunk, and that eventually the scent would wear off. I also told him I would be glad when it did.

December

Snow, snow, and more snow! That was the forecast in Assilem today.

In reality snow starts as rain and then freezes. Assilem is a little different. Snow starts as snow. The snow is a warm snow though. Once it goes into the clouds and passes through, it turns into a cool snow. Being in Ikkin with snow on the ground, this now made sense of how it snows but it is not a bitter cold snow.

Wow I would really enjoy snow in reality if it was like this. Big bulky clothes are aggravating.

I do love this land in the sky and I look forward to having many more *adventures here. Even Beast has learned that heights are not that bad.*

The true storyteller...Uncle George

www.ingramcontent.com/pod-product-compliance
Ingram Content Group UK Ltd.
Pitfield, Milton Keynes, MK11 3LW, UK
UKHW020216250726
13967UKWH00001B/24